HALO

GREEN PATROL

AMAZON

Written by Bali Rai

Illustrated by Margherita Ende

RISING ★ STARS

Hachette UK's policy is to use papers that are natural, renewable and recyclable products and made from wood grown in well-managed forests and other controlled sources. The logging and manufacturing processes are expected to conform to the environmental regulations of the country of origin.

ISBN: 9781398324268

Text © 2021 Bali Rai
Illustrations, design and layout © Hodder and Stoughton Ltd
First published in 2021 by Hodder & Stoughton Limited (for its Rising Stars imprint, part of the Hodder Education Group),
An Hachette UK Company
Carmelite House, 50 Victoria Embankment, London EC4Y 0DZ
www.risingstars-uk.com

Impression number 10 9 8 7 6 5 4 3 2 1
Year 2025 2024 2023 2022 2021

Author: Bali Rai
Series Editor: Tony Bradman
Commissioning Editor: Hamish Baxter
Illustrator: Margherita Ende/Astound US
Educational Reviewer: Helen Marron
Design concept: Julie Joubinaux
Page layout: Rocket Design (East Anglia) Ltd
Editor: Amy Tyrer

With thanks to the schools that took part in the development of *Reading Planet* KS2, including: Ancaster CE Primary School, Ancaster; Downsway Primary School, Reading; Ferry Lane Primary School, London; Foxborough Primary School, Slough; Griffin Park Primary School, Blackburn; St Barnabas CE First & Middle School, Pershore; Tranmoor Primary School, Doncaster; and Wilton CE Primary School, Wilton.

A catalogue record for this title is available from the British Library.

Printed in the United Kingdom.

Orders: Please contact Hachette UK Distribution, Hely Hutchinson Centre, Milton Road, Didcot, Oxfordshire, OX11 7HH.

Telephone: (44) 01235 400555. Email: primary@hachette.co.uk.

GREEN PATROL

Leader: Martha Singh
(supported by
Olive Summer)

Age: 13

Status: Billionaire

Company name:
HALO

GREEN PATROL MEMBERS

AYAN   MAX   SILVA   SHAN

HALO's objective: To carry on the work that
Martha's missing mum and dad started – to save wildlife
and to save the planet.

Enemy target: TITAN (HALO's enemy). TITAN is a
big company that puts wildlife and the environment at
risk. It makes money from environmental crime.

Is TITAN behind Martha's missing mum and dad …?

Next task: Code name: **Amazon**

Chapter 1

The Amazon rainforest, Brazil ...

Ayan and Max were following a man. He was tall with a scar on his cheek. He was driving a truck carrying toxic barrels to poison the Amazon River. TITAN were behind the plan. They were going to cut down the trees and frighten the local tribe and wildlife away.

"We can see him," said Max.

Ayan tapped her ear bud. "Green Patrol is all set!"

"Don't let him out of your sight," said Olive.

"We are too good for that," Ayan said.

Olive and Silva were staying with a local tribe, near the Amazon River.

"This is what we fight for," said Olive. "To save people, the wildlife, and the forest."

"We have to act, NOW!" said Silva.

"We will, kid," Olive replied. "This is what Green Patrol and HALO do."

Shan and Martha were hidden in the TITAN camp in the forest, not far from Olive and Silva. From there, they could see TITAN loggers with machines, cutting down tree after tree.

"It makes me feel like crying," said Shan. "Why are they doing this?"

"Money," said Martha. "They are after more money."

"But why destroy the trees?" replied Shan. "And the wildlife?"

"We are going to stop this," said Martha.

Shan kicked a stone angrily. "They can't do this!" she shouted.

Chapter 2

In the rainforest ...

Ayan and Max had one task. To stop the man with the scar. His name was Mr Jones. The children followed a track in the rainforest. Mr Jones had no idea they were after him.

Max updated Martha on his HALO phone. "He's going to the river."

"Okay," said Martha. "Stay with him."

"Do we stop him?" asked Ayan.

"No," Martha replied. "We stick to the plan. Later."

A yellow snake slid by.

"That's a pit viper," said Ayan. "Look out!"

The toxic snake slid slowly away.

"Mr Jones has stopped," said Max. The map on his phone showed a red dot.

"The track ends there," said Ayan. "He has to walk now."

"Good," said Max. "That will slow him down."

Now they had more time. They had to stop him. They could not fail …

Chapter 3

The tribe's village ...

Back at the tribe's village, Olive and Silva met with the leaders. Silva got a surprise – Olive could speak to them!

"You understand them?" he asked.

"Yes," said Olive. "They are old friends."

Just then, the chief came over. "Olive!" she said with a wide smile.

"Rosa, how are you?" said Olive.

"Not so good," said Chief Rosa in English.

"Is there a problem?" Olive asked.

Rosa told Olive that as the forest got smaller, the tribe had to keep moving.

"It's TITAN cutting down all the trees," she said, frowning.

Olive nodded. "I need your help."

"What do you need?" asked Rosa.

Olive opened a map on her HALO phone. It was filled with red dots. The loggers were getting closer.

"We have a plan," she told Rosa. Together, they were going to release a flock of protected, rare birds – sun parakeets. If they were released, TITAN had to stop what they were doing to the forest.

"Fantastic," Rosa replied.

Chapter 4

TITAN'S camp ...

Shan stayed hidden at the side of the TITAN camp. The loggers were nearly finished for the day. They might soon come back to their cabins.

Martha had crept over to one side of the camp.

"Stay alert," she said, speaking to Shan in her ear buds.

"It's still quiet," Shan replied.

"Good," said Martha. "I'll look around ..."

Martha waited a moment, then she ran behind a cabin and hid. Three TITAN workers appeared. They didn't see her.

When they went away, Martha quietly moved on.

The cabin doors had electronic locks. To enter, you had to put in a code.

"We need to hack the locks," Martha said in a whisper.

Shan crept to the nearest cabin. Her HALO phone helped her to hack the door lock. The door opened and Shan stepped inside. But just as she did so, the door snapped back. Shan tried the lock again, but it had jammed.

"Martha!" she hissed. "The door! It's stuck!"

Shan was trapped ...

Chapter 5

Back on the track, Ayan hid in the bushes. Max was behind her. They could hear Mr Jones muttering angrily. He had hoped to drive to the riverbank but now he just had to walk.

"I'll sneak around and see what's in the truck," said Ayan.

"Okay. I can still see Jones from here," Max replied. "Stay alert, Ayan!"

When it was safe, Ayan moved to the truck. One mistake and Jones would see her ...

Inside the truck were ten barrels. Each barrel had a big red 'TOXIC: POISON!' sticker.

"Ten barrels," Ayan whispered into her HALO phone.

"OK," Max replied. "Jones will have to carry them to the river, one by one."

"That means we have time to stop him," said Ayan.

But, they didn't …

Just as Ayan crept back into the bushes, another jeep arrived. Five TITAN workers jumped out.

"Get those barrels to the river!" Mr Jones shouted.

The men scowled but began their task. One of them looked over at the bushes. Ayan ducked and returned to Max.

"What now?" asked Max.

Chapter 6

The tribe's village ...

Chief Rosa showed Silva into the village school. It was a small hut, with no desks. A pile of old books sat in the corner.

"I left years ago, but returned to teach the children and help my people. Now, TITAN wish to destroy our forest," Rosa said.

"TITAN must be stopped," Silva replied.

"And we will help you," nodded Rosa.

Outside, Olive got updates from the Green Patrol team. Martha and Shan were still at the TITAN camp. Ayan and Max were following Mr Jones. Olive rang Martha.

"I can hear Ayan in my ear buds," Martha said. "Jones is taking poison to the river! We need to start our plan now."

"The forty sun parakeets from HALO are on their way," Olive told Martha.

"Fantastic!" said Martha. "But Shan is trapped. I'm going to try to get her out."

"Okay, we had better get moving then," Olive said – as Silva and Rosa joined her. "Has everyone been told what to do?" she asked.

"Yes," said Rosa. "My people live by the river. TITAN will get a big surprise ..."

Chapter 7

TITAN'S camp ...

Martha had to free Shan before the TITAN workers returned. She couldn't let the workers find Shan in the cabin, no matter what.

"Shan?" she whispered into her HALO phone.

"Yes?"

"Have you tried hacking the lock with your phone again?" asked Martha

"Yes!" said Shan. "I'm not silly!"

"Okay, okay!" said Martha. "Let me see what I can do from the outside."

Martha tried the door but it was stuck.

Next, she had a go at hacking the entry code. But it didn't help. She could have broken the lock, but the TITAN team would then see it.

"Hang on ..." Martha said. "Shan?" she whispered.

"Still here," said Shan. "Not like I'm going somewhere else!"

"I'm going to try to reset the door lock," said Martha.

"Will that help?" asked Shan.

"No idea," said Martha. "But I'm going to try."

Martha set her phone to scan. It soon took control of the lock. Martha cleared the code and turned the lock off. Nothing happened. She waited. Then she turned the lock back on again. The lock buzzed and then it opened with a clunk.

"YES!" yelled Martha.

As Shan escaped from the cabin, they could hear the sound of trucks and jeeps. The TITAN logging crew had returned.

"Hide!" said Martha. "When they are inside the cabins, we can trap them." She tapped her HALO phone screen.

Chapter 8

In the rainforest ...

Ayan and Max made their way to the river. It was getting late.

"I'll set up the cameras here," said Max, reaching into his backpack. Inside were five mini video cameras, shaped like spiders.

"Spider-cams are so cool!" said Ayan. "What clever person invented them?"

Max smiled. "Olive," he replied.

Max put out the spider-cams. Each one could film the riverbank without being spotted by Mr Jones.

"Let's go!" Max shouted.

With the help of her HALO phone, Ayan turned on the cameras. She checked each one. Every spider-cam was working. It was perfect!

"They are coming!" Max told her. "We need to hide!"

Mr Jones was barking orders. The men moving the barrels of poison sounded annoyed.

Ayan led Max back into the bushes. Now they had to wait ...

Chapter 9

The tribe's village ...

Silva saw the helicopter. The tribe's children stopped playing and looked up. The helicopter sounded like thunder.

The black HALO chopper soon landed and Silva marched over to meet the pilot.

"Forty rare birds," the pilot said, as he jumped out.

The sun parakeets were in bird cages. There were five wonderful birds in each cage. They had yellow, orange and green wings, with black beaks. "They're so cool!" said Silva.

"Be quick," said the pilot. "I've only got five minutes ..."

Silva nodded.

"Need a hand?" yelled Rosa.

The helicopter blades were still spinning.
Rosa, Olive and two more women came
to help. Soon, all of the cages were safely
off. The pilot left right away.

"He was in a hurry!" said Silva.

"TITAN track
the skies," said
Olive. "HALO
jammed their
signal, but not
for long. He
had to leave
before TITAN
found out."

"And now we
can set the parakeets free!" grinned Silva.

Chapter 10

TITAN'S camp ...

At the TITAN camp, Shan and Martha's plan had worked! The workers were locked in their cabins. It was time.

Shan slid under one of the trucks. In her hand was a small black box. She stuck it to the truck and slid out again. One down, six to go. Martha was doing the same. Soon, each truck got a remote-controlled black box.

Shan tapped her HALO phone. She slid her finger over the screen. Underneath the trucks, each box beeped to show it was armed.

"Now?" asked Shan.

"Now!" Martha told her.

Shan tapped the screen again. The boxes fizzed and buzzed.

"It's like giving the trucks an electric shock," said Martha.

"Really?" said Shan.

"Yes," said Martha. "The motors get fried. They won't start now."

One task down. One to go. Martha and Shan set off for the logging machines …

The tribe's village ...

Silva could see the sun parakeets flying up and away. The brightly coloured birds lit up the sky like fireworks. Chief Rosa filmed them on her phone.

"I'm sending this to the local police," she said.

"Will they stop TITAN?" asked Silva.

"They have to," said Rosa. "The birds are protected. TITAN are finished here. And we are safe."

Silva smiled. "We win!" he said.

"Not quite," said Olive from behind him. "We still have Mr Jones to deal with."

Chapter 11

In the rainforest ...

Mr Jones smiled. It was the smile of a bully. The barrels were at the riverbank. It was time.

"Open them slowly," he told his men.

One of the barrels was opened. Hidden in the bushes, Ayan and Max gasped.

"Now tip the barrel into the river," Mr Jones ordered.

But that did not happen. Suddenly, a band of tribepeople from the village appeared from out of the trees.

"WHAT IS GOING ON?" Mr Jones yelled.

Behind him, his men ran away.

Then, a siren sounded. It was a police speedboat ...

"NO!" Mr Jones shouted. "This isn't right!" He tried to run, but he couldn't. He was trapped by the tribe.

The police jumped from their boat and ran to get him.

Ayan and Max appeared from out of the bushes. Ayan smiled at Mr Jones.

"Hey!" she said. "Looks like your plan failed."

"No!" said Mr Jones. "You can't beat me. You are just kids!"

Max grinned. "We are not *just* kids, Mr Jones," he said. "We are Green Patrol!"

Chapter 12

Wiston Hall, England ...

Green Patrol sat in Martha's kitchen, eating pizza.

"So, they tried to poison the river?" asked Silva.

"Yes," Martha replied. "They make the mess and then they get paid to clean it up. It is disgusting!"

"And they carry on cutting down the rainforest," Olive added.

Max wiped tomato ketchup from his mouth. "That's TITAN," he said. "But *we* stopped them."

Max grabbed more pizza. "So, what next?" he asked.

The screen on the wall lit up. Ayan groaned.

"We've tracked smugglers to Hong Kong," Martha told them.

"What are they smuggling?" asked Silva.

"Snow leopards," said Martha.

"Then we have to stop them!" Shan said, jumping up from her chair.

"So, no rest again?" Ayan complained.

Martha grinned. "This is Green Patrol," she said. "We never stop. And we *never give up!*"

Chat about the book

1 Read Chapter 4. How did Shan get locked inside the cabin?

2 Ayan spotted a toxic snake in the forest. What does 'toxic' mean?

3 Go to page 9. Why was the forest getting smaller?

4 Go to page 27. Why did the author say the parakeets were like fireworks?

5 Read Chapter 11. How does the author make us feel about Mr Jones? What does he do and say?

6 Would you like to be a member of Green Patrol? What would it be like?